THE MOST INFLUENTIAL WOMEN IN THE ARTS

BREAKING THE GLASS CEILING
THE MOST INFLUENTIAL WOMEN™

THE MOST INFLUENTIAL WOMEN IN THE ARTS

AVERY ELIZABETH HURT

New York

For Olivia Buff, a female artist who is not destined to remain in the shadows

Published in 2019 by The Rosen Publishing Group, Inc.
29 East 21st Street, New York, NY 10010

First Edition

Library of Congress Cataloging-in-Publication Data

Names: Hurt, Avery Elizabeth, author.
Title: The most influential women in the arts / Avery Elizabeth Hurt.
Description: New York : Rosen Publishing, 2019. | Series: Breaking the glass ceiling: The most influential women | Includes bibliographical references and index. | Audience: Grades 7–12.
Identifiers: LCCN 2017050396| ISBN 9781508179641 (library bound) | ISBN 9781508179795 (pbk.)
Subjects: LCSH: Women artists—Juvenile literature.
Classification: LCC N8354 .H87 2018 | DDC 704/.042—dc23
LC record available at https://lccn.loc.gov/2017050396

Manufactured in the United States of America

On the cover: Artist Frida Kahlo stands at her Mexico City home and studio around 1940. She is renowned for her vivid paintings, which broke boundaries in race and class, as well as gender.

CONTENTS

INTRODUCTION

Deep in cool, dark, silent caves in southern Europe, Australia, and Asia are the earliest surviving examples of human art. During the Paleolithic period—roughly forty thousand to ten thousand years ago—our ancestors adorned the walls of caves with incredible images. Rich, vivid colors and an uncanny sense of motion give these paintings power even today. Herds of horses and reindeer and bison race across the cave walls, stalked by the ferocious predators who were ancestors of today's lions and tigers. Cave bears strut and prey cowers.

But more common than these beasts are the prints and stencils of human hands that fill the cave walls. Some scholars think the handprints were a way of signing the art: *I did this. This is my work.*

Or perhaps they represent something a little more existential: *Remember me. I was here.*

Whatever their meaning, when we look at these paintings today, we feel a strong connection with the ancient hunters who painted them and often a fierce desire to know more about those who lived and hunted and made art so long ago. Their art suggests that these artists were not so different from us.

And a close look suggests that the artists were not all men.

For many years, most scholars assumed that ancient cave paintings were exclusively the work of men. However, recently scientists analyzed these prints and determined that women made at least three-quarters of the handprints in Paleolithic cave paintings. We know little about these ancient people. But as we gaze at a picture of a gazelle in flight or a dying bison, we know that this most beautiful example of Paleolithic art was as likely, even more likely, to be the work of a woman as of a man.

She did the work. She left her mark. And for thirty-six thousand years people gave the credit to a man.

Of course, women have always made art—and received recognition. They made quilts to keep their families war, they made pottery to cook and serve food, and they made baskets and wove tapestries. They created songs to sing their babies to sleep and dances to celebrate marriages and mourn deaths. They wrote poems and stories to tell of their worlds and feelings. Their paintings decorated their homes. And sometimes their artwork was placed in galleries and reproduced in books, recognized and appreciated as being equal to and deserving of a place alongside art by men. Sadly, that hasn't happened enough. As in so many fields, women artists have struggled to be taken seriously. That hasn't stopped them, though. And while thirty-six thousand years of women artists have been underappreciated, they have not been without influence.

Whenever a modern human looks at those cave paintings and is moved to chills or tears, he or she is being touched by a woman, reaching through

Paleolithic handprints adorn a cave painting of a horse, in the Pech Merle cave in the village of Cabrerets, France.

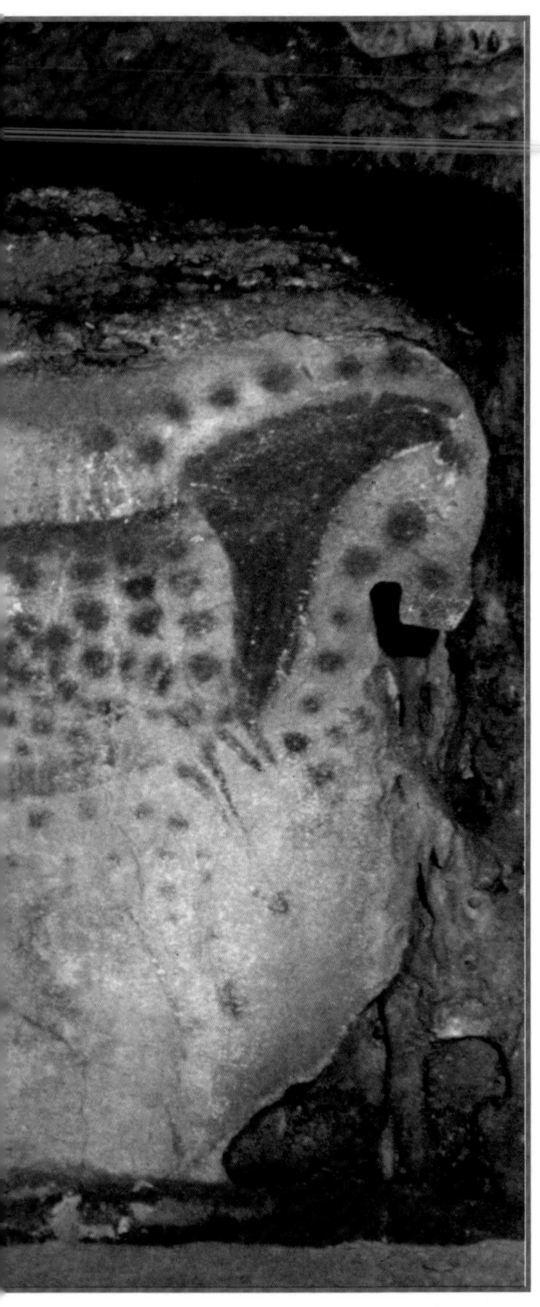

the millennia. Every painting that has been made since has owed something to these women as well as men for the techniques, the creativity, and the neurological changes that made possible representative art.

This resource covers many women artists from the ancients to today who have left their handprints on the world's art. Some got the credit they deserved; others did not. But in all cases, their work has influenced the men and women who came after. Even working in the depths of a dark cave, women artists found a way to say: I did this. I was here.

CHAPTER ONE

SHADOW PAINTING: ANTIQUITY

Pliny the Elder was a Roman scholar who lived in the first century CE. In his thirty-seven-volume encyclopedia, *Naturalis Historia*, he tells the story of a lovesick young woman who lived in Greece sometime around 600 BCE. She had fallen in love with one of her father's apprentices, but the young man was soon to go abroad. The night before the apprentice was set to leave, the young woman, Kora, drew on the wall the outline of her lover's face. The young woman's father, Butades, was a potter. He immediately recognized the beauty and power of his daughter's drawing. He filled in the lines with clay, creating what Pliny tells us was the world's first relief sculpture. When some people tell this story today, they say that the first artist was a woman. But it is not Kora, but Butades, whom Pliny

Dibutades, or *The Origin of Drawing*, painted by Joseph-Benoît Suvée in 1791, depicts Kora tracing her lover's face.

celebrates. The daughter, when she is considered at all, is remembered merely for inspiring her father's more important work. Kora, like her drawing, is just a shadow tracing.

Least Talked About

Of course, we know that the story is just a legend. People had been making art long before the ancient Greeks. The Greeks were not even the first to make relief sculpture. (Paleolithic people got there first, too.) And those who like to say that the first artist was a woman are giving Kora far more credit than Pliny did. But as a metaphor for women artists, it would be hard to find one better than the story of Kora and her drawing.

By the time of Kora and Butades, life had come a very long way since the days of the cave painters. This is the period known by scholars as Antiquity, and we have much more information to go on. Antiquity is generally considered the time after which history was being recorded but before the Middle Ages. For those of us who live in the West, it refers mostly to the Greeks and Romans and is also called the classical period. Of course, during this time people were living and making art in the rest of the world as well. But for now, let's talk about the Greeks and Romans—Pliny's people, as well as the people of Butades and of course his daughter.

Another historian, Thucydides of Greece, recounts a speech made by Pericles, a fifth-century BCE Athenian general and statesman. Pericles said, "The greatest glory of a woman is to be least talked about by men, whether they are praising you or criticizing you." Women obviously had their roles, but as Pericles makes clear, those roles had nothing to do with the dealings of men. Women did not vote, own property, or hold public office. This was not unusual at that time, nor was it particularly unusual in most of the world until the last century—and in many places it is still the way of things. Of course, in societies where women have no voice and no power, their work—no matter if it is art or some other kind of work—is usually not considered important.

Scorning the Duties

However, let's not be unfair to Pliny, who told the story of Butades and his daughter. In his *Historia Naturalis*, Pliny mentioned several female artists. Timarete lived in Athens in the fifth century BCE. Her father was a painter, and she took up his trade. As Pliny put it, "She scorned the duties of women and practiced her father's art." Among her works was a triptych of the goddess Diana that was kept in the temple of Diana at Ephesus. The painting was destroyed many years later when the temple was sacked. Pliny offers little detail of the other women painters he mentions by name. However, we know a bit about

A depiction of Timarete at her easel, a miniature from around 1400, is now displayed in the National Library in Paris.

a few of them. Iaia of Kyzikos (around 50 BCE) was known for portraits of women (including at least one self-portrait) and seems to have had a reputation for working very quickly. Some sources say that Iaia's work was valued above that of more famous painters working at the time and even sold for more money than more famous painters (the famous ones were, obviously, men). Anaxandra was a female painter working in the third century BCE. She is said to have painted mythological scenes.

AN ISLE OF WOMEN

Sappho is generally considered the greatest female artist of antiquity. She is certainly the one who gets the most attention today. She lived in the seventh century BCE, much earlier than Pliny, and even earlier than the women artists he mentioned in his encyclopedia. Sappho is mostly known for her poetry, though ancient texts refer to her work as songs. The few remaining works we have (often just scraps of poems) seem to have been written down after her death, suggesting that she performed them as songs, rather than writing them as poems.

Like most women who lived this long ago, little is known about Sappho. But there are many legends and stories. Sappho is today celebrated as a lesbian

(continued on the next page)

(continued from the previous page)

poet—in fact, the English word "lesbian" comes from Lesbos, the name of the island where Sappho lived. Her poems often celebrate the beauty and love of women.

Some stories say that Sappho established and ran a school on Lesbos that trained women in the arts, though recent scholars have questioned this. Some stories say she died young when she flung herself from a cliff after being spurned by a lover; others say she lived to be very old. Some of her poems mention graying hair and other facts of aging, so the latter story is possibly the correct one. Whether or not any of the stories about her are true, Sappho's remaining poems and the many legends about her continue to inspire artists—women and men, lesbian and not—even today.

This first-century CE fresco of a Roman woman poet has come to be called the Sappho portrait.

Helena of Egypt, daughter of Timon, lived around 400 BCE. She is thought to have painted *The Battle of Issus*, a depiction of the battle in which Alexander the Great defeated Darius of Persia. Though we do not know how remarkable a subject this was for a

This mosaic from around 1900 depicts the Battle of Issus, the subject of one of Helena of Egypt's paintings.

woman painter at that time, it seems likely that it was at least unusual. In more recent years (as we shall see), women artists, no matter their media, were expected to stick to subjects suitable for women. Children, flowers, and domestic scenes were considered appropriate subjects for the ladies—battles, not so much.

Besides a tidbit here and there, we know virtually nothing about these women, their lives, or their art. We are lucky to even know they existed. However, it is interesting that Pliny, and others, make occasional mention of women artists in this period, proving that while it may have been unusual for women of antiquity to make art and even to make money from their art, it wasn't unheard of either. In addition, some surviving artworks of the period depict women in the act of painting, suggesting that a woman at the canvas was more common than the mention of a mere six women artists might suggest.

Like the women who left their handprints in the caves, we can't know exactly how much and what kind of influence these women had. Like Kora, they and their work are mostly lost in the shadows. But by the medieval period, though we still know very few of their names, we start to see that they could be very influential on other artists and their societies.

CHAPTER TWO

ILLUMINATING NUNS: THE MEDIEVAL PERIOD

Life in medieval Europe was very different from life in the classical period, but in many ways, it was not much different for women. Women still had little or no social or political power. It was exceptionally rare for a woman to have a chance to get any education. Even most upper-class women were unable to read, and their education was limited to things that would be useful to a wife running a household. Women were, for the most part, expected to care for their husbands, their children, and their homes and communities. They were in all ways considered less important than men, and men were for the most part completely in charge of the women in their lives. Of course, this did not mean that women didn't work. Much of medieval society was rural, and women contributed by caring for animals; working in the fields with their husbands, brothers, and fathers; and baking, spinning thread, weaving fabric, and making fabric goods. When women did work for pay, documents from the period show that they were paid far less than men for the same work.

There were, however, two ways a woman might have some measure of financial and intellectual independence and some measure of control of her own life. If a woman inherited property from her father or her husband, she was allowed to own and control that property until she remarried. As soon as she remarried, anything she owned became the property of her husband.

The other way a woman might gain some power and even some independence was by becoming a nun. The church was a powerful institution in medieval Europe. Women with intellectual or artistic interests or talents were often attracted to the church, and many of them joined convents. In convents, women were not only able to get an education but they could also rise to positions of power within the church by becoming the abbess, or the head of a convent. In some cases, women even had authority over men (in convents that housed both nuns and monks). This option was for the most part open only to upper-class women, or at least women with some financial resources. Women joining a convent were expected to provide at least a small dowry to help cover the costs of housing them. Poor women sometimes joined convents or monasteries as servants. This certainly didn't give them any power or opportunity for advancement and precious little independence. It did, however, put their lives and fates in the hands of the abbess at a convent rather than the whims and quirks of husbands and fathers. Unlike the secular world, in which there was virtually no check on the ways a woman could be treated by her husband or father, the world of the convent had rules, routines, and traditions for the women who lived there. It was a haven of safety and security for many women.

Medieval nuns also made art. In fact, they were responsible for some of the most beautiful and

This medieval funeral pall was embroidered by nuns in about 1500 to be used as a decorative covering for a casket.

revered artwork of the period. One very important job for medieval nuns was to illuminate manuscripts that scribes and monks had copied. This meant that they drew decorations in the borders and beginnings of the texts and sometimes added small illustrations throughout the manuscript. They also did embroidery and tapestry.

We don't know the names of very many of these artists. This is in part because the individual was not considered as important in those days as now. Community was more important than individuals. This was even more the case in the church and in monastic orders, which were extremely communal societies. However, occasionally nuns (and monks) would sign their work. This was likely more as an identification of a person giving an offering to God rather than as an artist signing a piece of artwork, but it does help us to know who some of these women were.

Herrad of Hohenberg

Herrad of Hohenberg (sometimes called Herrad of Landsberg) was a nun and abbess in a monastery in the twelfth century in Alsace (in what is now France, at the borders of Germany and Switzerland, but at the time was ruled by Germany). As abbess, Herrad oversaw the production of *The Hortus Deliciarum*, or *Garden of Delights*, an encyclopedia for women.

This is a reproduction of one of the pages of the *Hortus Deliciarum*. Notice the pictures in the margins, a feature of illuminated manuscripts.

The *Hortus* was intended as a text for nuns to use for teaching younger nuns and novices. As such, the *Hortus* was filled with theology and morality lessons as well as practical information on the natural world. It was a compilation of texts by many different writers. The work was written mostly in Latin but occasionally had German definitions and explanations. Though the text of the *Hortus* includes some remarkable writing, it is appreciated mostly for its illuminations, or illustrations. Herrad wanted to make sure that the work was lavishly illustrated. She supervised a group of nuns in doing the artwork and made sure that the finished product was magnificent. Though the original was partially destroyed in a fire, copies of many of the images had been made; so today we can still see and admire the works of these mostly forgotten medieval women.

Hildegard von Bingen

Hildegard von Bingen is one of the best known of female medieval artists. She lived in the twelfth century and was a mystic and a Benedictine nun. Eventually, she became the abbess of a monastery in Bingen, Germany. She had visions from the time she was a small child. These included detailed scenes of the life of Christ and other religious themes, such as the relationship between God and humans. Eventually, years after taking vows, she began to

This illumination by Hildegard von Bingen depicts one of her many visions and interprets them through a biblical lens.

record these visions in writing. She also wrote many lyric poems, in addition to works of theology, medicine, gardening, and natural history (what today we would call science). Hildegard was also one of the contributors to the *Hortus Delicarium.* But she is probably best remembered for her music. She is the author of seventy-seven liturgical chants. She is admired even today for both the melodies and the poetry of her compositions.

STORYTELLING ON FABRIC

The Bayeux tapestry is one of the most famous examples of medieval tapestry. It tells the story of the Norman conquest of England. A series of seventy scenes are stitched in intricate embroidery on a piece of linen fabric. It is about 230 feet (70 meters) long and about 19.5 inches (49.5 centimeters) wide. The scenes are carefully stitched in several colors of thread. The main part of the tapestry tells the story, in order, of the conquests. The borders are filled with other, unrelated images: animals, scenes from Aesop's fables, and farming and hunting scenes. The end of the tapestry is missing, and the thread colors and the linen fabric itself have faded over the years, but it is still a beautiful piece of work that speaks to art lovers even today.

Ende

Ende was another illuminator of medieval manuscripts. She lived in the tenth century, well before Hildegard and Herrad. Though she was not as powerful and influential a woman as Hildegard and Herrad, we know about her work because she signed some of her pieces (though signing work was unusual at the time, it was not unheard of). Ende worked on a manuscript known as "Apocalypse of Gerona," which was written and illustrated in Spain, where she lived. Ende signed some of her work "God's helper." Another work she signed "female painter." We cannot know why she chose to put these signatures on her work, but signing "female painter" gives us the impression that she wanted to be sure the world knew that the painting was done by a woman.

CHAPTER THREE

THE WORLD IS A BIG PLACE: NON-WESTERN ART

So far on our tour of women's art through the ages, we have been talking about art in the West—mostly Europe. Art is and has been made all over the world. People have made art in Africa, Asia, the Middle East, Australia, and the Americas at least since Paleolithic times. So let's take a look at what was going on with women and art in a few non-Western traditions.

Unsurprisingly, women, as far as we know, didn't fare much better in other places than they did in the West in the distant past. Women were second-class citizens in most of the world until surprisingly recent times. Of course, as we've seen, this doesn't mean women weren't making art. Sadly, it does mean that their work was often ignored or belittled. Although most women artists in the premodern period remain anonymous, we know a few by name, though we know little about their individual biographies. However, in later periods, and places around the world, a few women left not only their handprints but their names as well.

Premodern African Art

Because Africa is most likely the cradle of humankind, you would assume that some of the oldest art would be found there. And you'd be right. There are many examples of ancient rock art that date as far back as the cave art in Europe, if not farther. In later periods, sculpture, beadwork, carved masks, textiles, and other forms of art appear in various places on the African continent. Like in the caves of Europe, it is difficult to know why these works were done. Were they strictly decorative, or did they have some social, religious, or even practical purpose? And of course, we cannot know the individuals who made them. It is highly likely, however, that many of these early makers were female. Like medieval European society, societies in Africa were predominantly agricultural. Most societies were organized by clans, and clan leaders were mostly men. Women did have important roles, though. Women were at least sometimes, and perhaps even usually, spiritual leaders. Because in premodern times art was often an expression of religion, this makes it likely that women were responsible for at least some of the art, and maybe a great deal of it. But like the classical and medieval artists of Europe, we know very little about these individuals.

Islamic Art

In the Middle Ages (while nuns were illuminating manuscripts in Europe), Islamic culture was flourishing. The period from the seventh to the thirteenth centuries is known as the golden age of Arab civilization. Learning and culture flourished in an Arab empire that stretched from Spain to the border of China. Beautiful architecture, great literature, and innovative science were hallmarks of the Arab world during this period. Because Muslim tradition forbids representing living beings in art, the most

The courtyard of the University of Al Quaraouiyine in Fez, Morocco. The university was founded by Fatima al-Fihri.

common forms in Islamic art are architecture, poetry, and mosaics.

As in Europe, women in Islamic cultures were not allowed much power, but they did play a bigger role

CALLIGRAPHY

Calligraphy literally means "beautiful writing" and is not the art of composing poems and stories but the practice of artistically rendering words and letters on the page.

Calligraphy has long been one of the most valued art forms in many Asian and Middle Eastern cultures. In addition to mathematics, Arab cultures place great value on language and the written word. Practicing calligraphy is a way of honoring the written word. As such, calligraphy is an important part of Islamic art. In China and Japan, the power of the word is also greatly respected, and calligraphy is one of the major art forms in both countries.

It is a mistake to think of calligraphy as merely decorative—as just a way to make party invitations and wedding announcements more attractive. Traditionally, calligraphy is considered a means of expression very much like poetry. Examples of calligraphy in China date back to the Shang dynasty, roughly 1600 to 1100 BCE. Artists in many cultures, both Eastern and increasingly Western, still practice the art today.

than many people think, particularly during the golden age. The Muslim world had its share of powerful women like Hildegard. In the ninth century in Morocco, a Muslim woman, Fatima al-Fihri, founded the world's first university. But we know very few female artists from the early days of history. One we do know a little about is Lalla Arifa. Arifa was a Muslim poet living in India in the fourteenth century. Like the women we learned about in the last chapter, Arifa was a deeply religious woman. She became a Sufi, which is a Muslim mystic. Her poems were mostly about ordinary household activities, but she used these as metaphors for her relationship with God.

Japan

Japan has a history of respect for women artists. For centuries, upper-class women took painting supplies—brushes and paints—with them when they married. However, just as in Europe, it was not until the last century or so that women were able to get an education, which would allow them to pursue art as a career. However, daughters of artists and art teachers were able to learn from their fathers.

Kiyohara Yukinobu, who lived from 1643 to 1682, was a fairly well-known Japanese female artist. She was the daughter and granddaughter of famous painters of the Kano school of painting. She worked within that tradition but also added some of her own touches and became well known and much respected

This delicate painting of quail and millet was painted by Kiyohara Yukinobu in the late seventeenth century.

among her colleagues. Her work has recently been rediscovered and exhibited in Japan.

China

Guan Daosheng made a name for herself during the Yuan dynasty in China. She lived from 1262 to 1319. Although women were generally not well educated at this time in China, Guan came from a prosperous family and was educated in many subjects, including art. Her husband was also a painter, and they are said to have had a fruitful artistic partnership. They influenced and inspired one another and are thought to have worked together on some paintings. Because her husband was a government official, Guan was able to travel widely. This was unusual for a woman and provided Guan with plenty of ideas for her paintings and calligraphy. Guan was a Chán Buddhist, and her work reflects Buddhist influence. She worked in calligraphy and often painted bamboo, a common subject for male painters, but one considered inappropriate for women. Unusually for a woman of the period, her work was recognized and honored during her lifetime.

CHAPTER FOUR

FOLLOWING IN FATHER'S FOOTSTEPS: THE RENAISSANCE (1300–1600)

The Renaissance began in Italy and quickly spread throughout Europe. It's difficult to pin down an exact date, but the medieval period ended and the Renaissance began sometime around the fourteenth and fifteenth centuries. It was a time when people became very interested in classical (Greek and Roman) learning. The word "renaissance" means "rebirth" and refers to a rebirth of classical learning. Medieval art was made primarily by and for the church, and its subjects were typically religious. During the Renaissance, the primary subject of art shifted from biblical stories to the stories of Greek and Roman mythology and other secular subjects. Portraits and other representational art became common during this period.

Life for women changed somewhat during the Renaissance as well. Women were still completely subject to their husbands or fathers and had little to no political rights. But the attitude toward women did subtly change. Women were valued, but only if they kept their place, and that place was highly restricted. Women were expected to be modest and passive, virtuous and loyal. Their sphere was motherhood and the family. Women were expected to keep out of the public eye, and men were discouraged from discussing business and political affairs with the women in their lives.

Some scholars have made the case that during the Renaissance women had even less power than they had during medieval times. A loosening of feudal bonds and the rise of capitalism gave men more economic and educational opportunities. Not only were these opportunities not extended to women but they made it easier for men to keep women dependent on them. Women could not get jobs outside of the home, and men no longer needed them to help with the farmwork or other family business.

Nuns (and monks) still made devotional art, but as the interest in secular art grew, there were more opportunities for artists outside the church. Not surprisingly, those opportunities were limited mostly to men. As more men outside of monasteries began painting and composing music, those forms of art began to be seen as "men's art," while needlework and other fabric arts were seen as women's art or domestic arts. Women's art—or crafts, as these

Self-portrait by Sofonisba Anguissola. This was completed around 1556 and is now in a museum in Łańcut, Poland.

things came to be known—was devalued and, to a degree, is still treated as less serious and less valuable than other forms of art. Nevertheless, just as in previous times, Renaissance women did make art, and some of them were quite successful at it.

The Renaissance was anything but a rebirth of women's art, but what we do find in this period are women artists whose names and stories we know and whose influence is still appreciated today.

Sofonisba Anguissola

One of the first well-known female artists of the Renaissance was Sofonisba Anguissola. She was born in Cremona, Italy, in 1532 to a noble family. Unlike most other successful female artists of the time, her father was not an artist. When she was a young woman, her father sent her to study with a local portrait artist. In turn, she taught her younger sisters to paint. This not only gave Anguissola artistic training but it made it more acceptable for other Italian artists to accept female students. After her father wrote to Michelangelo about his daughter, the great painter sent some of his own drawings to her to copy. She returned her copies and Michelangelo critiqued them.

Anguissola specialized in portraits and was known for the detail, rich colors, and expressiveness of the eyes in her paintings. As one of the first, if not the very first, successful female artists, she became something of a celebrity in her day and influenced other young women to become painters.

THE HEART OF A KING

The Renaissance came to England later than to the rest of Europe, and the English Renaissance is better known for its writers (anyone heard of Shakespeare?) than its painters and composers. England during its Renaissance was home, however, to the greatest breaker ever of a glass ceiling. Elizabeth I of England was not the first woman to rule a country (not even the first to rule England; her sister Mary has this honor, although her rule was brief). However, Good Queen Bess is generally considered the greatest ruler, male or female, England has ever had. She was also a talented writer and a great patron of the arts. In one of her most important speeches, she said, "I know I have the body of a weak and feeble woman, but I have the heart and stomach of a king." History has shown, however, that Elizabeth I was anything but weak and feeble.

Queen Elizabeth never married. If she had, she would have remained queen, and her husband wouldn't have been king. But he would have ruled the country. Why? Because in those days, a woman had to obey her husband, even if she was the queen! Disobeying your husband was a crime. (Elizabeth's sister and predecessor tried, not too successfully, to get around this problem by marrying Philip, who was already the king of Spain). Elizabeth, however, was clever not to marry, even though that created the problem of who would succeed her, since she had no children. In the end, she passed her throne to her cousin, James IV of Scotland. He became James I of England and was not nearly as good a ruler as Elizabeth.

Queen Elizabeth I, around 1565. Elizabeth I was both a writer and a patron of the arts. She also looked great in a ruff.

Francesca Caccini

Francesca Caccini was the first woman to compose an opera. Her father was also a composer. Francesca was born in Florence, Italy, in 1587. She was a talented singer and played many instruments, including harp, lute, and keyboard. She also taught singing. Along with her mother and sisters (who were all talented singers), she performed at the court. But it is her work as a composer that is most impressive. Her compositions were well known and highly valued at the time. She turned down several lucrative job offers, including one from Henry IV of France, because she preferred to stay in Florence. Some of her works have survived. Her opera, *La liberazione di Ruggiero*, is still occasionally performed.

Lavinia Fontana

Fontana was born in Bologna, Italy, in the late sixteenth century. Her father was a successful painter and art teacher who worked in Florence, Rome, and Bologna. He taught Fontana to paint. But perhaps more importantly, he provided her with exposure to the works of many other major painters. The local nobles often commissioned Fontana to paint their portraits. She did not limit herself to portraiture, however. She also painted religious works, including altar art for churches. She is thought to have produced more pieces of art

Lavinia Fontana's oil painting *Jesus Appears to Mary Magdalene*. It was painted in 1581 and is now in the Galleria degli Uffizi in Florence, Italy.

than any other woman up to that time. Though she is remembered primarily for her religious work, her portraits may have had a greater influence on other painters. She is known for an uncanny ability to capture the personality of her subjects.

Not only did Lavinia Fontana break ground as a female painter but she was ahead of her time in her lifestyle as well. Her husband, Gian Paolo Zappi, was also a painter, who had been taught by Fontana's father. But after their marriage, Zappi managed the household (which included eleven children!) and limited his artwork to painting backgrounds and frames for the paintings of his more talented and successful wife.

Caterina van Hemessen

At this point, you may be getting the idea that Italy was the only place in the world where one could find paint and brushes or instruments for making music. Of course, Italy was not the only place where people made art in those days. But it was the place where the Renaissance of art and learning began and took hold. That is why so many of the great Renaissance artists—the ones who have such an influence over artists even today, such as Michelangelo, Raphael, and Botticelli—lived there. But the Renaissance did reach to the rest of Europe. Influential Renaissance artists also include Jan van Eyck in the Netherlands and Albrecht Dürer, born in what is now Nuremberg,

A Lady with a Rosary, a miniature portrait by Caterina van Hemessen, painted around 1550. Now in the National Gallery in London.

Germany. And yes, we find an occasional woman working in other lands during this period. Caterina van Hemessen was born in Antwerp, Belgium, in 1528. She painted small portraits, some of which have survived. She was not as innovative as some other artists, but she was extremely successful. Miniature portraits were quite popular at the time, and van Hemessen painted many of these for wealthy and royal patrons. She is credited with painting the first self-portrait of an artist at work. In it, she is sitting at the easel, looking out toward the viewer, as if she is being patient with an interruption to her work. It's interesting that the first self-portrait of a woman artist at work shows her being interrupted (and not complaining about it).

There are no records of work by van Hemessen after her marriage, and sadly, many art historians believe that she gave up her art when she married.

These women don't get the top billing of their male colleagues. But we now know that at least a few women artists of this period also left their marks and influenced later artists. And as we move on through history, we'll find a gradually increasing number of women artists. As the arts grew to include more theater and dance and eventually photography and film, we'll see that women contributed to these arts as well. But next, let's take a look at how women got ahead of their male colleagues as the art of the Renaissance began to change.

CHAPTER FIVE

COMING TO LIFE: THE BAROQUE PERIOD (1600–1750)

Social and political life didn't change much for women between the Renaissance and the period we'll discuss in this chapter. But art did change, and women artists were often ahead of the curve in this change. The Baroque period in Europe spans roughly from 1600 to 1750. During this period, artists introduced a sense of movement and excitement into their works. It seemed as if the subjects in the paintings might at any minute speak or move. Even still-lifes had more vitality. The peel of a lemon hangs off the table or flowers are shedding blossoms. Music, too, was livelier with more variations of meter and style.

The exact border between Renaissance and Baroque art can be fuzzy. It's often unclear to which period a given painting or piece of music belongs.

Caterina van Hemessen self-portrait. Here the artist manages to capture both the spirit of the Renaissance and the Baroque—and probably the spirit of the artist as well.

This is especially difficult when it comes to women artists. Elements we think of as Baroque begin turning up in women's art a little earlier than we might expect. Remember Caterina van Hemmesen's self-portrait? It's an otherwise very Renaissance style, but she is looking up from her work as if, at any moment, she just might sigh and ask, "What is it *now*?" That's so Baroque! So let's look at a few other women painters and composers who helped change the world of art—and one or two who began to change what it meant to be a female artist.

Artemisia Gentileschi

Gentileschi exemplifies the Baroque spirit as well as any artist, male or female. She was born in Rome, Italy, in 1593. Her father was also a painter. When her father recognized his daughter's talent, he hired another painter, Agostino Tassi, to teach her. Around 1612, after what seems to have been a fairly long period of sexual harassment, Tassi raped his young student. He was convicted after a sensational trial. Like many rape victims, then and today, Gentileschi was subject to a great deal of humiliation during the court proceedings. She was accused of being promiscuous and subjected to a vaginal examination.

Gentileschi's experience with Tassi (both before the rape and because of it) seems to have had an influence on her art. One of her more famous works is

Judith and Holofernes by Artemisia Gentileschi. This powerful painting is in the Galleria degli Uffizi in Florence, Italy.

a painting called *Susanna and the Elders.* The painting depicts the biblical story of a virtuous young woman being sexually harassed by religious leaders. Men who tackled this subject often portrayed Susanna as flirtatious. Gentileschi, however, shows a clearly frightened Susanna being bullied by leering and threatening men. This painting was completed before the rape but may have been influenced by Tassi's sexual harassment of his young student before he finally raped her.

Gentileschi's painting of the story of Judith and Holofernes was almost certainly done after the rape and possibly during the trial. It makes an even more powerful statement. Judith was a Jewish widow who rescued her town from an invading army. The story goes that Judith got the enemy leader, Holofernes, drunk and then, with the aid of her maid, beheaded him. In her painting, Gentileschi graphically portrays the beheading, not only showing the brutality of the murder but the intense concentration on the faces of the women. They are holding Holofernes down. The maid is leaning in as Judith puts all her strength into pulling the sword across the man's neck. Their hands are covered in blood. It is easy to imagine that Gentileschi was thinking of Tassi when she painted this scene. A painting on the same theme, by Gentileschi's contemporary Caravaggio, depicts Judith and her maid as being a bit squeamish, leaning back and away from their victim. Gentileschi's women show no such reserve.

Gentileschi's story has a happy ending, however. Not long after the trial, Gentileschi married and moved to Florence, where she continued her education as an artist. She was the first woman to be admitted to the Florentine Academy of Fine Arts. After separating from her husband, she was in the rare position of being in control of her own life and household. She and her daughters, who were also artists, spent many years moving around Europe following career opportunities.

Elisabetta Sirani

Several of the women we've discussed so far taught other women to paint—usually their sisters or daughters. Elisabetta Sirani, however, was the first to establish and run a painting school for

The Baptism of Christ by Elisabetta Sirani (1658). Sirani pioneered a woman-owned and -run painting school and was the first woman to support herself and her family with her art.

women. She is also one of the first female artists (that we know of) to support herself and her family totally through her art. She was born in Bologna, Italy, in 1638 and lived there all her life. She was an accomplished portrait artist and teacher and was known for being able to paint very fast. This no doubt helped her make a living painting. She didn't limit her artistic energies to painting, however. She was also a printmaker and a musician.

Sirani's story does not have a happy ending. She died unexpectedly after having terrible pains in her stomach. Her father suspected that one of the servants had poisoned her, but nothing was ever proven. Modern scholars suspect the cause of death may have been ruptured stomach ulcers caused by working too hard.

Elisabeth Jacquet

Elisabeth Jacquet was born in Paris, France, in 1665. Her family was very musical, and many of them were instrument makers as well. Elisabeth was a musical prodigy. She played the harpsichord and sang. She performed at the court of the French king Louis XIV when she was still in her teens and continued to write and perform music throughout her life. She was well known in her time, particularly for her marvelous improvisations on the harpsichord. But where Jacquet really broke the glass ceiling was in opera. She was the first female composer to have an opera performed in France.

AREN'T WE MISSING SOMETHING HERE?

Why no dancers? Why no architects? Why no sculptors? When we think of the arts, we generally think not only of painting and music but also of dancing and theater, of architecture and sculpture. During this period, women artists were often noted, in some cases even celebrated, for their contributions to arts such as needlework and painting. In other fields, it took much longer for women to gain entry.

Because women were expected to stay out of the public sphere, art forms such as architecture and sculpture were mostly closed to women then (and, of course, women we considered far too delicate to be carving marble). Careers in theater and dance were unavailable to women because those lifestyles were considered immoral. Women who did get involved in theater were generally thought of as not much better than prostitutes. It was many years before theater came to be considered a respectable career for a woman.

Geertruydt Roghman

Geertruydt Roghman was an engraver, born in Amsterdam, Netherlands, sometime around 1650. She is remembered for a series of engravings of women doing household chores—sewing, spinning, cleaning, and so on. Her work doesn't seem exactly groundbreaking until you take a close look. Men who were doing similar work at the time put a great deal of detail into the people they portrayed, even when those people were household servants (and not rich art patrons). Conversely, Roghman's household scenes were quite dreary. In her paintings, women were typically portrayed with their backs to the viewer. They seemed to have no individuality at all. It may be a modern interpretation, but it is difficult not to see Roghman's engravings as a statement on the status of women and the value placed on their work.

Maria Sibylla Merian

The artists discussed so far have worked mainly as painters or composers (a few did engravings, printmaking, and musical performances). Maria Sibylla Merian was born in 1647 in Frankfurt am Main, Germany. When she was young, she began a caterpillar collection so that she could watch them change into butterflies. She grew up to be an illustrator who specialized in detailed renderings of insects and plants. These were not just charming nature drawings (such as might have been expected of female painters). They were scientifically accurate illustrations to aid students of entomology.

Somewhat like Gentileschi, Merian became a rare example of a woman living an independent life.

This 1675 illustration of a rose by Maria Sibylla Merian includes close scientific detail, as well as botanical notes.

After divorcing her husband in or about 1691, she and her daughter (who was also an artist) traveled to Suriname in South America, where they could observe and study types of insects and plants that were different from those that could be seen in northern Europe. She later published a book called *The Metamorphosis of the Insects of Suriname*, which contained illustrations of the different stages of development of Suriname's insects.

CHAPTER SIX

FINDING THEIR VOICES: THE NINETEENTH CENTURY

The nineteenth century provided both hope and a dilemma for women artists. On the one hand, there were far more opportunities for them, including new genres (such as photography). On the other hand, women were still under a great deal of pressure to focus on their homes and families and to not pursue careers, artistic or otherwise. Nevertheless, far more women were making their mark in the arts than ever before.

A majority of well-known women artists of the Renaissance and Baroque periods were from Italy. In the 1800s, England became a particularly fertile ground for female artists. Queen Victoria was an enthusiastic patron of the arts. She worked hard to increase the visibility and improve the status of English artists, whether male or female. American women also made impressive gains as arts professionals during the nineteenth century.

Women still did not have many rights or much political power, but they were finding their voices. Women in England and in the United States began increasingly to organize and attend meetings and rallies to support the temperance and abolition movements. By the end of the century, the crusade for women's right to vote was well underway.

As their voices began to be heard in the public square, more and more women began to express themselves in the studio, in the dark room, and on the stage.

Sarah Bernhardt

"The Divine Sarah" to her many fans, Sarah Bernhardt was the first internationally celebrated actress. She was born in Paris, France, in 1844. During her long career, she played many roles on stages all over the world. She appeared in Europe, the Americas, Australia, and the Middle East.

Though she was already fifty-six at the turn of the century, Bernhardt fits better in the twentieth—or even the twenty-first in some ways—than the nineteenth. She was exceptionally good at being a celebrity. She promoted herself with a skill that rivaled her talent for acting, using her sometimes-outrageous personal life to grab the public's

Sarah Bernhardt was known for playing male roles, including the title role in William Shakespeare's famous play *Hamlet*.

attention. She had a series of notorious affairs with wealthy and powerful men. She remained independent, however. She owned and managed her own theater company and introduced many innovations in theater. She was renowned for several roles in which she played men, including the title role in *Hamlet*.

Sarah Bernhardt broke a lot of glass ceilings during her life. She was the first woman to appear crossed-dressed in a film, the first woman to die in a film, and, perhaps more significantly, the first woman to commission her own role in a film.

CARTOONING FOR THE CAUSE

Getting women the right to vote took a lot of work (and wasn't accomplished in most countries until the middle of the twentieth century). Women marched, made speeches, and wrote lots of letters and newspaper editorials. However, art played a role, too. Posters and editorial cartoons that championed the cause of women's suffrage were popular, especially in England and the United States. Many of the artists who worked on these cartoons and posters were women. The jokes and images that helped convince

(continued on the next page)

(continued from the previous page)

the world that women deserve an equal voice in government seem familiar today, a hundred years later. In one cartoon, Uncle Sam is portrayed as a woman; in another, suffrage leaders Elizabeth Cady Stanton and Susan B. Anthony are shown sitting in heaven on either side of George Washington. The cartoon is meant to evoke a similar painting in the Capitol Rotunda. The Rotunda painting shows Washington being taken to heaven surrounded by women who represent Liberty and Victory. We don't think of editorial cartooning as being influential in the history of art, but it most certainly influenced the ability of women to make art and have their work taken seriously.

Mary Cassatt

Mary Cassatt was born in Pennsylvania in 1844 but trained and lived much of her life in France. She was a painter and printmaker who became friends with Edgar Degas, one of the leaders of the French impressionist movement in art. Her style was quite modern and innovative. Her subjects, however, were more traditional. Male impressionists often painted large scenes of people in public places, on picnics or in cafes. Because she was a woman, Cassatt was expected to stick to domestic settings. She

The Child's Bath by Mary Cassatt. This painting is now at the Art Institute of Chicago in Chicago, Illinois.

painted women and children in the midst of their daily lives. One of her most beloved works is a painting of a mother bathing her child. Many of her paintings feature mothers and children. For this reason, critics have often belittled her work as being "feminine" and therefore less serious than similar work by men. However, Cassatt's skill is unmistakable. Her paintings also show a depth of understanding of her subjects that other works of the period lack.

Like Bernhardt, Cassatt understood the business side of her art. She developed relationships with dealers and collectors in Europe and in North America. She was a major force in the spread of impressionism beyond France.

Harriet Powers

As we saw in the last chapter, needlework, being an art practiced mostly by women, had long been considered a lesser art. (Deciding what were the lesser and what were the greater arts was, of course, an activity practiced mostly by men.) Harriet Powers, however, unequivocally proved that the fabric arts are worthy of being called great art. Powers was born a slave in the US state of Georgia in 1837. After emancipation, she and her husband worked a farm near Athens, Georgia. There she made quilts and displayed them at fairs in the area. At a cotton fair in Athens in 1886, an art teacher and collector discovered Powers's work.

This cotton appliqued pictorial quilt was created by Harriet Powers and is now in the Museum of Fine Arts in Boston, Massachusetts.

Handmade quilts were common in the South at that time (and still are). Many of them are extraordinary pieces. Powers's work, however, was something special indeed. She used a combination of European quilting traditions and West African textile arts to tell stories. Her stories were drawn primarily from the Bible and West African folktales. Her quilts were too small to cover beds or be used as blankets. This suggests that they were intended as works of art to be displayed rather than as useful household goods. Only two of Powers's quilts have survived. One is in the Smithsonian's National Museum of American History; the other is at the

The Hopi-Tewa potter known as Nampeyo is shown here displaying some of her art, which combined traditional designs and modern styles.

Museum of Fine Arts in Boston, Massachusetts.

Nampeyo

Nampeyo was a Hopi-Tewa potter who lived on the Hopi reservation in Arizona. Her name means "snake that does not bite." Though the artist herself may have been quiet, her pottery definitely got some attention. Nampeyo showed tremendous skill in shaping and decorating her pieces. She also developed new techniques for firing her work. At the time she was working, the Hopi people were beginning to use more manufactured kitchenware and had less need of traditional pottery. This didn't slow down Nampeyo.

Instead, this development helped her transform pottery from a handicraft to an art form. She incorporated traditional, prehistoric designs into modern works and created a new and exciting style.

Around 1875, Nampeyo found a market off the reservation for her ceramics. This gave her more resources to experiment and further improve her techniques. This also introduced her to a wider audience. Her work was mostly unsigned but widely collected. Her pieces are distinctive enough that collectors are usually able to identify them with ease. Nampeyo taught her art to her children, grandchildren, and other family members. Many of them have carried on making ceramics in a style similar to Nampeyo's. Other artists have been influenced by her as well.

Caroline Louisa Daly

For 125 years, six of Caroline Louisa Daly's paintings hung in prestigious Canadian art galleries. The only problem was, they were attributed to two different men named Daly, one Charles, the other Corry. It took a century and a quarter for the female artist to get credit for her work. Daly was born in Canada but

Caroline Louisa Daly might have been recognized sooner if she'd signed her paintings with her name instead of her initials.

traveled widely and lived in both Canada and England. Her paintings are watercolors, generally of ships and ocean scenes. She signed her work "C. Daly," or "C. L. Daly," perhaps explaining the confusion. However, it is telling that when trying to determine the person responsible for these beautiful watercolors, the true artist was overlooked, while men—one of whom wasn't even an artist—were assumed to have painted them. Fortunately, Daly's grandson and the curator of an exhibit featuring Daly's work discovered the error and gave credit where credit was due.

CHAPTER SEVEN

I AM WOMAN: THE TWENTIETH CENTURY

The twentieth century was a very good one for women. By the middle of the century, most women in most nations had the right to vote and hold public office. Hand in hand with this were changes in attitudes about women. Women had far more independence, freedom, and opportunities than they had ever had before. They still struggled for true equality, though.

The 1960s and 1970s saw the birth of the women's movement. Now that women had the right to vote and a greater say in the affairs of their countries, they began to demand equality in all aspects of life. Equal opportunities and equal pay for equal work were their primary demands. And they made a great deal of progress. By the end of the century, it was no longer difficult to find women working in the arts, and no field completely excluded them. However, pay equality was proving challenging, and glass ceilings were still frustratingly tough to break.

By the last decade of the twentieth century, women held only 17 percent of directing, writing, and editing jobs on the top-grossing films. Women were only 7 percent of directors of these big-name films.

Things were even worse for women in the visual arts. Women were woefully underrepresented in commercial galleries and in the directorships of museums. The three most prestigious art museums in the world (the Louvre in Paris, the British Museum in London, and the Metropolitan Museum of Art in New York) had no female directors during the century. (As of this writing, they still have not.) H. W. Janson's *History of Art* is one of the most widely used and widely respected surveys of art history. It is often used in college art classes. The 1980 edition of this popular text featured zero women artists. That's right. Zero. The book gave readers the impression that women did not exist in the art world.

In classical music, change also moved at a glacial pace. By the middle of the century, most major orchestras had hired at least a female player or two. Nonetheless, the percentage of females in major orchestras still hovered in the single digits. Here again, that glass ceiling was stubborn. Female conductors were even rarer than female players.

Even when women artists were recognized for their work, they struggled to be taken as seriously as men. Lee Krasner was an exceptionally skilled painter and one of the founders of the abstract expressionist school of art. Her art instructor once said of one of her paintings, "This is so good you wouldn't know it was done by a woman."

Though female artists were still struggling, they were no longer quiet. Just like their cave-painting sisters, modern women were leaving their handprints all over the place.

Georgia O'Keeffe

Georgia O'Keeffe once said, "The men liked to put me down as the best woman painter. I think I'm one of the best painters." No one any longer describes O'Keeffe as "the best women painter." She is undoubtedly one of the best painters of the twentieth century, male or female, and one of the most influential.

O'Keeffe is well known, even among people who know or care very little about art. Her insistence on living her life her own way, as well as doing her art her own way, inspired a generation of feminists.

In the nineteenth century, women painters seemed trapped in painting subjects that were considered acceptable for women: domestic scenes, children, flowers. O'Keeffe painted flowers, too. But what flowers she painted! When it first became obvious that O'Keeffe was a painter to contend with, many in the male-dominated art world suggested that if she wanted to be considered a real painter, she

Georgia O'Keeffe, shown here about 1931, did not limit her work to so-called "women's" subjects. She painted large-format flowers and bones, like this skull, as well as cities and landscapes.

should paint bigger subjects. Her response was to paint bigger flowers: huge close-up renderings of gorgeous flowers. Many art critics have seen these as representations of vaginas, though O'Keeffe denied any such intention. That hasn't stopped other women artists as seeing O'Keeffe's flowers as a validation.

The writer and journalist Joan Didion had this to say about Georgia O'Keeffe, "Like so many successful guerrillas in the war between the sexes, Georgia O'Keeffe seems to have been equipped early with an immutable sense of who she was and a fairly clear understanding that she would be required to prove it." And prove it she did. Today people who care about art recognize O'Keeffe as one of the most powerful and inspirational of modern artists.

Annie Leibovitz

During the 1970s and 1980s, Annie Leibovitz worked as a photographer for the American magazines *Rolling Stone* and *Vanity Fair.* It was while working for these magazines that she developed her unique style of portrait photography. She used bold colors and unique, sometimes outrageous poses to capture her subjects. Her photographs conveyed not only her subjects' personalities, but also their place in the larger culture. She photographed the actress Whoopi Goldberg in a bathtub of milk, the actor Sylvester Stallone posed as Rodin's famous sculpture, *The Thinker,* and actress Demi Moore nude and pregnant. That photo created controversy at first, but in the end helped pregnant women feel less awkward about their bodies. Leibovitz's portraits captured the spirit of the times. They make a remarkable statement about life in the turbulent twentieth century. In 1991, Leibovitz became the first woman to have her work exhibited at the National Portrait Gallery in Washington, D.C.

Although much of Leibovitz's work is iconic of the twentieth century, she is still pushing boundaries and practicing her art.

Frida Kahlo

In 2017, the painting *Dos desnudos en el bosque (la tierra misma)*—"Two Nudes in the Forest (the land itself)" in English—sold for $8 million dollars. It was the work of a Mexican artist named Frida Kahlo and was the most

Annie Leibovitz, shown here standing before some of her portraits, was the first woman to show her work in Washington, D.C.'s National Portrait Gallery.

ever paid for a work by a Latin American artist. Unfortunately, Kahlo's work did not sell this well while she was alive.

Kahlo had polio when she was a child and was severely injured in a bus accident when she was a teenager. Multiple fractures left her in a body cast. It was while recuperating that she began painting. Many of Kahlo's paintings depicted her battered and broken body. In addition to physical pain, her paintings often explore emotional pain. This was

CRAFT OR ART?

Historically, much of the art made by women were art forms that came to be called craft rather than art. These were often discredited and undervalued. But in the last century, that has begun to change. Ceramics and fabric arts, such as weaving, quilting, and knitting, are at last getting the respect they deserve. Twentieth-century feminist artists such as Harmony Hammond and Faith Wilding incorporated what were generally considered women's crafts, such as knitting and crochet, into their art. Faith Ringgold, a feminist artist and civil rights activist, began making what she called story quilts. These incorporated images and handwritten text to convey a narrative. Ringgold's use of craft techniques in her art served to further blur the distinction between art and craft.

often occasioned by the difficult relationship she had with her husband, the painter Diego Rivera. Though she suffered and portrayed that suffering in her art, Kahlo was anything but weak. She often dressed in male clothing and was openly bisexual in a time when that was not an easy life.

She was also brave and groundbreaking when it came to her art. At the time, it was typical to paint women as idealized subjects, good mothers, loyal wives, Madonnas. Kahlo was one of the first to portray female lives as they were actually lived. Her paintings depicted childbirth, breastfeeding, and abortion. Many of her paintings are self-portraits. She managed to paint her own pain without ever portraying herself as a victim.

Augusta Savage

Augusta Savage began making art when she was still a child. She sculpted figures from the red clay of her native northeast Florida. After her family moved to Palm Beach, she had to seek out new sources of clay. She found some with a local potter and continued to sculpt. Savage sold some of her sculpture at a county fair. Her work was well received, and she moved back to north Florida and tried unsuccessfully to establish herself as a sculptor. She made busts of prominent black members of the community there. However, she did not find enough work to make an adequate living. In 1921, when she was twenty-nine years old,

Augusta Savage, shown here working on one of her sculptures, was an influential model for men and women during the Depression.

she moved to New York to attend art school. She later studied art in Paris and other European cities. After returning to New York, she became a leader in the flowering of black culture and art known as the Harlem Renaissance. Among her most powerful works were a bust of scholar W. E. B. Du Bois and one of black nationalist Marcus Garvey. She was the first African American to be elected to the National Association of Women Artists. She founded a teaching studio in New York during the Depression and was very influential to a generation of artists, both male and female.

CHAPTER EIGHT

THE FUTURE IS FEMALE: THE TWENTY-FIRST CENTURY . . . SO FAR

During the twentieth century, female artists struggled for recognition. They also struggled to find their voices and the courage to use them. Georgia O'Keeffe painted in defiance of what "the men" said she should paint. Augusta Savage fought discrimination against her race as well as her gender. Frida Kahlo gave voice to bisexual and lesbian women and boldly painted things women had not previously been able to mention in public. By the end of the century, women were no longer quiet, no longer submissive.

Women are still struggling in the twenty-first century. Women still make less money than men. They are still a small minority in government and are still underrepresented in most of the arts. But things *are* different. The women's movement of the latter half of the previous century took women's issues from the fringe to the mainstream. Women artists working in the twenty-first century are, for the most part, less a part of that movement than beneficiaries of it. Today's female artists are addressing more than the bread and butter and lifestyle aspects of the feminism their elder sisters forged. They have turned their sights to economic and social justice. They are concerned with environmental justice and racial justice. Female artists of the twenty-first century work in a wider variety of media and represent more diverse cultures than ever before. It's too early to predict the lasting influence of these women. But one thing is certain: female artists are here to stay. And so is their work.

Mariko Mori

One of the most exciting things about recent art is how genres have expanded—and blended. Mariko Mori was born in Tokyo, Japan, in 1967. In her artwork, she doesn't limit herself to one genre. Mori creates films, photo murals, installation pieces, and performance art. She doesn't even limit her individual pieces to one form. When attending art school in London, she asked her teachers why there were no sewing machines in the sculpture department.

Her pieces incorporate sci-fi themes, fashion, traditional Japanese rituals, spirituality, and technology. She often inserts her own image into

Mariko Mori standing in front of her work, *Connected World,* at her exhibition "Rebirth" at the Royal Academy of Arts in London, England.

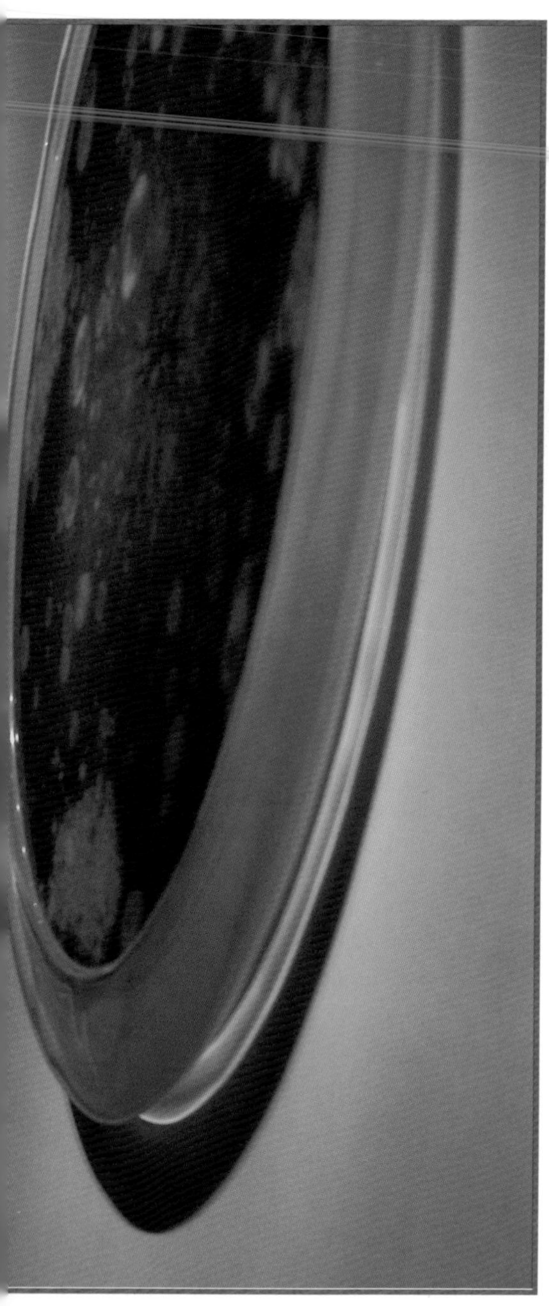

her work but with a twist. In one panoramic photo, she appears as a futuristic mermaid. Sometimes she appears as a cyborg. Her work has a powerful dreamlike quality and explores what it is to be human in the twenty-first century.

Shirin Neshat

Male domination of women has lessened a great deal in the West in the past one hundred years. However, in some countries in recent years, things have gotten worse, not better, for women. The 1979 Islamic Revolution in Iran replaced an open, democratic, and intellectual Persian culture with an oppressive regime that silenced dissent.

Iranian photographer and filmmaker Shirin Neshat poses for a photo at the London Film Festival on October 9, 2017, in London, England.

And silenced women. Shirin Neshat is an Iranian photographer and filmmaker. Because of her country's repression of speech and of women, she has chosen not to live there. She has lived most of her adult life in self-exile in the West.

In a 2010 TED talk, Neshat discussed the difficulties and responsibilities of being an artist in exile from repressive regimes. She embraced the role artists play in maintaining their cultures and questioning—even defying—governments that try to silence them. Artists, she said, are the "communicators" of their people. Throughout her career, Neshat has used images of women to explore political and cultural changes. In 2009, she made a film called *Women without Men*. The film explores the issue of being a woman in Iran and depicts what Iran was like before the revolution. Still, Neshat says that she yearns to make art that transcends the political.

Tauba Auerbach

The twenty-first century is still young. Many of the artists working today were still young at the turn of the century. Tauba Auerbach was born in San Francisco in 1981 and was only nineteen in 2000. She had her first solo art exhibit when she was only twenty-four years old. Auerbach is one of only a few women working in abstract art. Her work often deals with mathematical concepts. She has come a long way, indeed, since the days when women were expected to stick to domestic subjects.

You won't find many feminist statements in Auerbach's work, but she is not removed from social and political concerns. She publishes much of her art in the form of publications—books. She does this in part to make her work affordable. It is also an attempt to change the model of how art is bought and sold. Auerbach's beliefs about issues such as income inequality and greed are opposed to the values and practices of the art world. She wants plenty of people, not just the very wealthy, to be able to afford her art. So she began experimenting with a business model that would put her art in the hands of more people. More importantly, it would change the way art is consumed and marketed.

It may not sound like a big deal, but it is revolutionary for the art world. Today's female artists are using their voices to speak out not just for women but for everyone.

Kara Walker

Like so many of the women artists in the Renaissance and Baroque periods, Kara Walker followed her father into the business of art. Walker works in a variety of media—painting, printmaking, video animation, installation art, and collage. She is best known for her giant cut-paper silhouettes that caricature stock figures from the antebellum South.

FEMINISM BY ANY OTHER NAME

Though in the twenty-first century, many young women are uncomfortable with the term "feminism," most have internalized the movement's most basic beliefs and goals: women should be offered the same opportunities as men. When they do work of equal quality, they should be rewarded with the same pay and honors as men. Women should be allowed autonomy over their lives and bodies. Women should have the same access to education, employment, health care, and personal safety as do men. Women should have a voice in the public discourse and a role in the governing of society. Those basic aims are clear and have not changed even as the women's movement has matured. Art made by young women does not always have obvious feminist themes. That does not mean these female artists are not concerned about the issues women face. Perhaps it means that the philosophical argument has been won—even if some of the practical goals are still a ways from being achieved.

Her work deals with themes of race, gender, and identity. Her pieces are powerful and often disturbing. An article in the *New Yorker* says, "In Walker's work, slavery is a nightmare from which no American has yet awakened." Walker has received criticism from both racists and from blacks who feel that she has misrepresented them. Nonetheless, she has used her art to bring attention to the stereotypes, violence, and dehumanization that characterize America's racial history.

Zaha Hadid

It took women much longer to break into architecture than the other arts. But when they broke in, they made an impression. In 2004, Zaha Hadid, an Iraqi-British architect, was the first woman to win the valued Pritzker Prize for architecture. She scooped up many more prestigious awards as well. Hadid is recognized as one of the greatest architects of the modern age. Her work was experimental and has been called visionary. The London newspaper *The*

Zaha Hadid stands in front of the redeveloped Serpentine Sackler Gallery located in Hyde Park in London, England.

Guardian once referred to Hadid as "The Queen of the curve."

She designed London's aquatic center for the 2012 Olympics and the Guangzhou Opera House in China. Hadid died of a heart attack in 2016, but her work continues to influence and inspire a new generation of female architects.

Still Making Art

It's far too early in the twenty-first century to speculate about which artists working today will have the greatest influence in the years to come. But it's fair to say that many of them will be women—far more than in any past time period. Some of the younger women working in the arts today are exploring the same feminist territory as their older sisters. But most have expanded the revolution that made their work possible to take in other issues.

Nina Chanel Abney uses her paintings to explore race, gender, and politics. Her most recent exhibition focuses on the tension between the police and the black community. Nigerian artist Ifeoma Anyaeji creates sculptures and installation pieces out of found material, including nonbiodegradable plastic bags and bottles. Rachel Rossin, an American painter and programmer, combines art and technology to explore the intersection of physical and virtual reality. Laura Bird, a potter who lives in London, makes useful ceramic pieces that also tell stories. There is no field of art that is no longer open to women's creativity.

In the first few chapters of this book, we had to look long and hard to find women artists. And then we often did not know their names. It was difficult to learn their stories. In this chapter, there is not nearly enough room for all the women artists who are breaking barriers and boundaries and using the voices that were for so long repressed. The struggle of female artists has been difficult and is by no means over. Yet there has never been a better time for young women who feel the calling to make art. There are still many glass ceilings to break, but women have been smashing cracks into them since the days of the cave painters. They cannot hold much longer. And meanwhile, women are filling the world with art.

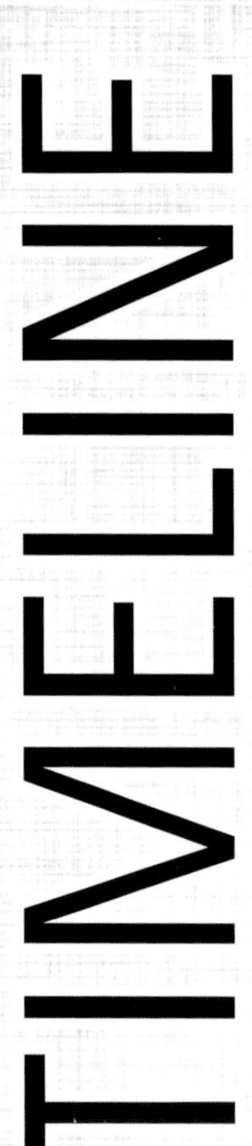

Paleolithic Era Decorative paintings and engravings were made on rocks in Africa. These are believed to be among the first examples of art.

Paleolithic Era Prehistoric peoples paint elaborate scenes on the walls of caves. Cave art is generally considered the first examples of art.

1600–1046 BCE Ancient Chinese people carve and paint calligraphy on animal bones.

77 CE Greek historian Pliny the Elder begins writing the multivolume encyclopedia *Historia Naturalis.* He mentions several early female artists in this work.

1070 CE (approximately) The Bayeux tapestry is created. The 70-meter-(230 ft) long tapestry tells the story of the events that led to the Norman invasion of England.

1185 The *Hortus Delicarium* is completed. The *Hortus* is an elaborately illustrated text covering a variety of topics, both spiritual and secular, that was used for the instruction of novice monks and nuns.

Eighth to thirteenth century The golden age of Islam. During this period, culture, learning, and art flourishes throughout the Islamic world.

Fourteenth century The Renaissance begins in Italy. The European Renaissance marks the end of the medieval period and the beginning of the modern period. It was a time of great culture and art and a renewed interested in and reverence for classical art and learning.

1533 Elizabeth I becomes queen of England. She was a devoted patron of the arts and a talented writer.

1830–1840 The techniques of photography are developed, leading to a new art form.

1848 The US suffrage movement begins in Seneca Falls, New York.

1920 The United States gives women the right to vote.

1917–1935 The Harlem Renaissance. This is a cultural, social, intellectual, and artistic explosion of black culture.

1960s/1970s to the present The modern women's movement works to extend the gains made by women in the previous century to include more rights, opportunities, and protections for women.

GLOSSARY

abbess The female leader of a convent or abbey of nuns.

autonomy Being in charge or allowed to be in charge of one's own life or circumstances.

BCE Before the common era or before the Christian era, used of dates before the year 1.

CE Common era, used of dates beginning with the year 1 in the Gregorian calendar.

cyborg A human who has mechanical or technological parts built into his or her body.

dowry The money or land (or other value) that a woman brings to her husband or husband's family when she marries.

embroidery The art of stitching decorative designs on fabric.

existential Relating to or concerned with existence.

feudal A government or social system in which nobles were given land in exchange for service to the monarch, and peasants worked the land in exchange for a portion of the produce.

illuminate To illustrate or decorate, usually with bright colors and intricate designs.

liturgical Having to do with the rites and ceremonies of worship, especially of Christian worship.

medium The form used by an artist, such as paint or clay.

mosaic A piece of artwork made by arranging small pieces of tile or glass to create a pattern or image.

mystic A person who tries to achieve unity with God or the absolute by contemplation or other practices.

neurological Relating to the brain and its functions.

novice A beginner, especially one who has recently joined a convent or monastery.

Paleolithic Having to do with the earliest period of the Stone Age.

representative art Art that depicts reality, particularly natural reality, such as people, plants, and animals.

secular Having to do with worldly, as opposed to religious, concerns.

shaman A spiritual leader who uses ritual, trance, and magic for divination and healing.

tapestry A heavy piece of fabric decorated with patterns or images and often used as wall coverings.

FOR MORE INFORMATION

American Women Artists
PO Box 755
Lodi, CA 95241-0755
Website: http://www.americanwomenartists.org
Email: contact@americanwomenartists.org
Facebook: @AmericanWomenArtists
Twitter: @Amwomenartists
Instagram and Pinterest: @amwomenartists

This nonprofit organization is dedicated to the encouragement and celebration of American women (from the United States and Canada) in the visual fine arts. The group works to increase the number of professional opportunities for women artists. The site has an extensive gallery of works by female artists working today.

Canadian Women Artists History Initiative
Digital Image and Slide Collection
EV Building, Room 3.741
Concordia University
1455 De Maisonneuve Boulevard West
Montreal, QC H3G 1M8
Canada
(514) 848-2424 ext. 5170
Email: cwahi@alcor.concordia.ca
Website: http://www.cwahi.concordia.ca

This is a great source for scholarly information on Canadian female artists. In additional to educational resources, this site includes an artist database with biographical information.

Georgia O'Keeffe Museum
217 Johnson Street
Santa Fe, NM 87501
(505) 946-1000
Website: http://www.okeeffemuseum.org
Facebook: @georgiaokeeffemuseum
Twitter, Pinterest, and Instagram: @okeeffemuseum
The O'Keeffe Museum in Santa Fe, New Mexico, offers information on the works as well as the working process of Georgia O'Keeffe. In addition to a collection of O'Keeffe's work, the museum offers a variety of educational and cultural events.

Girls' Art League (GAL)
1139 College Street
Toronto ON M6H 1B5
Canada
(416) 827-9739
Email: admin@girlsartleague.com
Website: http://www.girlsartleague.com
Facebook and Instagram: @girlsartleague
Twitter: GALeague
This Toronto organization works to empower and encourage girls of all skill levels and socioeconomic backgrounds to develop their

artistic voices. The group offers courses, workshops, artist talks, mentorship programs, and portfolio development for teenage girls. Classes are local, but the site provides links to web pages of female artists and feminist art groups.

National Museum of Women in the Arts (NMWA)
1250 New York Avenue NW
Washington, DC 20005
(800) 222-7270
Website: nmwa.org/explore/collection-highlights/16th–17th-century
Facebook, Twitter, Instagram, and Flickr: @womeninthearts
The NMWA is the only museum in the world dedicated solely to celebrating the work of women artists. The site includes profiles of artists, information about exhibits, and resources for students and teachers.

Women in the Arts
7512 Dr. Phillips Boulevard, Suite 50-635
Orlando, FL 32819
Email: womeninthearts@gmail.com
Website: http://www.womeninthearts.org
Facebook: @womenintheartsinc
Twitter: @WomenintheArtsc
This nonprofit organization strives not only to "celebrate the genius of women," but also to educate and promote the work of female artists,

educate people of all ages about women in the arts, and inspire young women to pursue the arts.

Women in the Arts and Media Coalition
244 Fifth Avenue, Suite 2932
New York, NY 10001
(212) 592-4511
Website: http://www.womenartsmediacoalition.org
Facebook and Twitter: @WomenArtsMedia
Pinterest: womenartsmedia
This group is made up of several organizations working together to empower women in the arts and media by networking, mentoring, and other forms of support. Coalition affiliates include academic art programs.

Women's Art Association of Canada
23 Prince Arthur Avenue
Toronto ON M5R 1B2
Canada
(416) 922-2060
Email: administration@womensartofcanada.ca
Website: http://www.womensartofcanada.ca
Facebook: @ WomensArtAssociationOfCanada
Twitter and Instagram: @womensartofcan
This organization is dedicated to advancing education in the visual, musical, and performing arts. In addition to funding scholarships, the organization offers education and resources to the public.

FOR FURTHER READING

Ball, Heather. *Astonishing Women Artists*. Toronto, ON: Second Story Press, 2007.

Bonney, Grace. *In the Company of Women: Inspiration and Advice from over 100 Makers, Artists, and Entrepreneurs.* New York, NY: Artisan, 2016.

Danneberg, Julie. *Women Artists of the West: Five Portraits in Creativity and Courage*. Pasadena, CA: Fulcrum, 2002.

Gold, Susan Dudley. *Kathryn Bigelow* (Great Filmmakers). New York, NY: Cavendish Square Publishing, 2014.

Greenberg, Jan. *Runaway Girl: The Artist Louise Bourgeois*. New York: NY. Abrams, 2003.

Hamilton, Tracy Brown. *Cool Careers without College for People Who Love the Arts*. New York, NY: Rosen Publishing, 2017.

Marciniak, Kristen. *Women in Arts and Entertainmen*t. Minneapolis, MN: Essential Library, 2016.

Osier, Peter. *Islamic Art and Architecture* (The Britannica Guide to Islam). New York, NY: Britannica Educational Publishing, 2018.

Reef, Catherine. *Frida and Diego: Art, Love, Life*. Boston, MA: Clarion Books, 2014.

Weidemann, Christiane. *50 Women Artists You Should Know*. New York, NY: Prestel, 2017.

BIBLIOGRAPHY

Als, Hilton. "The Shadow Act: Kara Walker's Vision." *The New Yorker*, October 8, 2007. https://www.newyorker.com/magazine/2007/10/08/the-shadow-act.

Chadwick, Whitney. *Women Art and Society.* 5th ed. London: Thomas Hudson, 2012.

Chicago, Judy, and Edward Lucie-Smith. *Women and Art: Contested Territory*. New York, NY: Watson-Guptill, 1999.

Clement, Clara Erskine. *A History of Art for Beginners and Students*. Project Gutenberg e-book, March 2008.

Cozzolino, Robert (ed). *The Female Gaze: Women Artists Making Their World*. Philadelphia, PA: Pennsylvania Academy of the Fine Arts, 2012.

Curtis, Gregory. *The Cave Painters: Probing the Mystery of the World's First Artists*. New York, NY: Knopf, 2006.

Davies, Caroline, et al. "'Queen of the Curve' Zaha Hadid Dies Aged 65 from Heart Attack." *The Guardian*, March 31, 2016. https://www.theguardian.com/artanddesign/2016/mar/31/star-architect-zaha-hadid-dies-aged-65.

Dobrzynski, Judith. "The Grand Women Artists of the Hudson River School." Smithsonian, July 20, 2010. https://www.smithsonianmag.com/arts-culture/the-grand-women-artists-of-the-hudson-river-school-1911058.

Gordenker, Alice. "Painting Women of Japan." *The Japan Times*, June 2, 2015. https://www

.japantimes.co.jp/culture/2015/06/02/arts/painting-women-japan/#.WdJjfTLMyiI.

Heartney, Eleanor, et al. *After the Revoluation: Women Who Transformed Contemporary Art. Munich*, Germany: Prestel, 2007.

Heller, Nancy. *Women Artists: An Illustrated History*. New York, NY: Abbeville Press, 1987.

Janson, H. W. *History of Art*. New York, NY: Abrams, 1968.

Kassam, Ashifa. "19th Century Female Artist Finally Gets Credit for Work Attributed to Men." *The Guardian*, February 1, 2017. https://www.theguardian.com/world/2017/feb/01/caroline-louisa-daly-art-men-attribution.

LaFrance, Adrienne. "The Weird Familiarity of 100-Year-Old Feminism Memes." *The Atlantic*, October 26, 2016. https://www.theatlantic.com/technology/archive/2016/10/pepe-the-anti-suffrage-frog/505406.

Mendelsohn, Daniel. "Girl, Interrupted: Who Was Sappho?" *The New Yorker*, March 16, 2015. https://www.newyorker.com/magazine/2015/03/16/girl-interrupted.

Nuwer, Rachel. "Ancient Women Artists May Be Responsible for Most Cave Art." Smithsonian.com, October 9, 2013. https://www.smithsonianmag.com/smart-news/ancient-women-artists-may-be-responsible-for-most-cave-art-1094929.

Poggioli, Sylvia. "Long Seen as a Victim, 17th Century Italian Painter Emerges as a Feminist Icon." NPR, December 12, 2016. http://www.npr.org

/sections/parallels/2016/12/12/504821139/long-seen-as-victim-17th-century-italian-painter-emerges-as-feminist-icon.

Quinn, Bridget. Broad Strokes. *15 Women Who Made Art and History* (In that Order). San Francisco, CA: Chronicle, 2017.

Thurman, Judith. “First Impressions: What Does the World’s Oldest Art Say about Us?” *The New Yorker,* June 23, 2008. https://www.newyorker.com/magazine/2008/06/23/first-impressions.

Walter, Chip. “First Artists.” National Geographic, January 2015. http://ngm.nationalgeographic.com/2015/01/first-artists/walter-text.

Waxman, Olivia B. and Liz Ronk. “Rattlesnakes and Ladders: The Inside Story of a Visit with Georgia O’Keeffe. *Time*, March 31, 2017. http://time.com/4702372/georgia-okeeffe-photographs-story.

INDEX